THE ADVENTURES OF THE
HUSKY PUPPY
SNOW DAY!

HEATHER MARIE

THE ADVENTURES OF THE

HUSKY PUPPY

SNOW DAY !

It's been two months since the Halloween party and Zeus has become close friends with Nicholas the dalmatian, Lily the golden retriever, and Sam the German shepherd. At recess, Zeus runs around as fast as he can as everyone tries to chase him, then they dig for buried treasure in the sandbox.

They have a lot of fun learning from Miss Molly, who teaches them about math, science, nature, spelling, and good manners. Zeus has really come to love science because they get to do science experiments.

As the weather turns colder, Zeus and his friends look forward to seeing some snow. Zeus loves the snow because he comes from a long line of snow dogs called huskies. His grandfather was famous for his speed. He used to pull sleds that delivered medicine and food to people in need. Zeus is named after him because he is so fast. He can't wait to run through the snow!

One day, Miss Molly, their teacher, says that she has a special surprise for them on the first snow day of the year. Zeus and his friends can hardly contain their excitement.

"What's the surprise?" Nicholas, the dalmatian pup, asks Miss Molly.

"Yeah, please tell us!" says Lily.

Miss Molly looks at the class with a smile. "Okay, I'll tell you. On the first snow day of the year, I always meet my students here at school for some fun science experiments. We make maple syrup snow candy that everyone can eat! And this year, I think I want to try to make a snow volcano."

The whole class gasps. A snow volcano! Candy! It sounds like the best snow day ever!

Zeus is excited.

"Today we're going to be learning about New Year's celebrations around the world," says Miss Molly.

Lily raises her paw.

"That sounds like fun!" she says when Miss Molly calls on her. "At my house, we make silly hats for everyone to wear on New Year's Eve, and then we throw them into the air when the clock strikes twelve."

"That's a great idea," says Miss Molly. "Lily, why don't you help me hand out paper, scissors, glue, and glitter to each student and you can show us how to make them!"

The class spends the rest of the day making their party hats while Miss Molly makes decorations for the New Year's party. Zeus and his puppy friends are excited, but they can't stop thinking about a snow day.

The whole class is preparing for a New Year's celebration party. There will be a big party with lots of food and games, and everyone is excited as they plan for the big day.

They learn about how New Year's is celebrated around the world, and Zeus and his friends enjoy seeing pictures from other countries as the people there celebrate and have their own parties. Miss Molly shows them pictures of people dancing and of colorful fireworks exploding over tall buildings. Zeus thinks it looks like a lot of fun.

The day before the party, it snows. Their little town is covered in sparkling white snow, and the roads are too icy for school to be in session, so the pups get a snow day! Yay! When Zeus wakes up, he stands at the window for a long time, looking out at all the snow. It covers the ground so completely that he can't even see the sidewalk!

"School is canceled today, little pup," his mama says. "You get your first snow day today!"

Zeus jumps up and down and wags his tail excitedly. Then he bundles up in his snow gear and he and Mama walk to the park, where his friends are already playing in the cold.

"Zeus!" says Nicholas. "Come and build a snow puppy with me!"

The day is cold but clear. The sun is shining and warming up the top of Zeus's furry head as he works in the snow. Together with Nicholas, he rolls up large balls of snow to create the body and head of a pup. They add ears, a nose, and eyes using leaves and rocks. When they are finished, the pups stand back and admire their work.

"He looks real!" Nicholas says.

"I bet he's really brave, too," says Zeus. "And I bet he's as fast as the wind."

"Well, hello there," says a voice.

Zeus turns to find Miss Molly standing there, bundled up in her bright purple coat and red hat.

"Hello Miss Molly!" Nicholas says. "We built a snow pup!"

"I see!" says Miss Molly. "You've done a fantastic job!"

"Are we going to do some experiments now?" Zeus asks.

"Not yet," Miss Molly says. "You keep playing and have some fun. I'll meet you at the school when you're finished."

The pups don't have to be told twice. They find Lily, who has brought several sleds for everyone to use, and they all take turns skidding down the biggest hill in the park. Then Zeus runs laps around the trees, going in circles so fast that he looks like a dark blur against the snow. Again, the other pups cheer, "Zeus on the loose, Zeus on the loose!"

This has become a common chant when Zeus really starts running. After that, Zeus, Nicholas, Lily, and Sam have an epic snowball fight that only ends when Lily loses her hat. Everyone stops what they are doing to help her look for it.

Mama turns around and says "Where's my little husky pup?" Just like that, Zeus zooms from across the park to run to his mama.

"Here I am!" Zeus says.

"I saw you running out there, little pup," Mama says to Zeus. "You looked just like your grandfather." Zeus is so proud; he puffs his chest out a little. He is named after his grandfather, after all, and it always makes him feel good to hear that he's fast, too.

"This is the life!" Zeus said.

When everyone is tired of playing in the snow, Miss Molly announces that she's ready to go to the school for her experiments. Zeus and Nicholas really aren't tired but they are willing to take a break to do science experiments with their other puppy friends. Zeus and his friends walk together, tumbling through the snow and kicking it up with their paws to see it sparkle in the sun.

When they arrive, Miss Molly boils maple syrup in a pot on a small camping stove. She tells the students to make fun shapes in the snow, such as paw prints and nose prints.

When the syrup is hot, Miss Molly carefully pours a little bit into each shape in the snow. The hot syrup and the cold snow react with one another, turning the syrup into pieces of hard candy in the shapes of noses and paws. When it's all done, everyone takes a piece to eat. Zeus has never tasted anything so yummy.

"SNOW CANDY!" Sam, the German shepherd shouted. Sam is usually the quiet one, but he really loves snow candy.

When the candy is gone, Miss Molly has the students work together to build a big volcano shape in the snow. The class becomes a team, pushing and packing the snow until it's the right size. When Zeus stands next to the volcano, it is taller than him!

Next, Miss Molly mixes some ingredients—water, baking soda, red food coloring, and soap—in a bowl. Carefully, she pours the mixture into the hole at the top of the volcano.

"Okay," says Miss Molly. "Everyone take a small cup of vinegar, and when I give you the signal, pour it into the volcano and stand back!"

Zeus and his friends take their cups and get ready. Miss Molly does a countdown: "Five, four, three, two . . ."

"One!" she cries with a laugh.

Everyone pours their vinegar into the volcano and BOOM! Out comes the red lava in a giant spray. It looks just like a real volcano erupting! Zeus and his friends stand back and watch as it spouts into the air.

"This is so much fun," Zeus says to Nicholas. "Snow days are the best!"

THE ADVENTURES OF THE HUSKY PUPPY

When the volcano is finished erupting, Miss Molly begins to clean up the mess. Everyone pitches in to help, and soon the job is done.

When Mama comes to pick up Zeus, she has some news.

"The snow isn't finished yet," she says. "There's more coming tonight, so there will be no school again tomorrow."

"Oh, no!" cries Lily. "Our New Year's party is tomorrow! We worked so hard on the decorations," she says sadly.

Zeus and Nicholas are excited for another snow day, but they, too, have been looking forward to the party. They say as much to Miss Molly.

"As for the party," Miss Molly goes on, "Leave it to me. I have an idea. It'll be a surprise."

Miss Molly and Mama talk privately for a moment, and then everyone goes their separate ways to head home for the day.

The next morning, Zeus tumbles out of bed excitedly and looks out the window. The snowfall has grown so much that the trees are heavy with it, bending their branches toward the ground. He can't wait to see his friends and go sledding, have snowball fights, and build snow puppies again.

"What's the surprise?" he asks, tail wagging back and forth.

"Get dressed and come with me," Mama says.

They bundle up again and walk toward the park. The snow is so thick, Zeus can't run as fast as usual because his paws keep sinking down!

All of a sudden, they hear a fire truck racing down the street, sirens blasting and horns honking! They look up, and there he is: Nicholas, the dalmatian, the Fire Pup! He is all suited up, and driving the firetruck!

Nicholas chanted, "Zeus on the loose, Zeus on the loose!" to support his best friend and he laughs and waves to his friends as the firetruck races by.

Zeus says in a proud voice, "Wow! Nicholas really is a firefighter! Cool!"

The pups are now bursting with excitement. When Zeus and Mama reach the park, Zeus can see and hear his friends shouting and having fun. They slide down the hill and at the bottom is the class party.

Table after table is set up with food, games, treats, and hot cocoa. One table holds all the sparkly hats the class had made for the party. Decorations are everywhere: sparkling streamers hang from the trees, balloons are tied to the branches, and confetti twinkles on the tables.

"How did this happen?" Zeus asks in wonder.

"Yesterday Miss Molly spoke to me about how we could give your class the party you had planned, even if school was canceled," Mama says. "So, she brought all the decorations out here, and I called all the mamas to see if they could help out."

Zeus looks around. There is Nicholas and his Uncle Ryan having a warm cup of cocoa with marshmallows. They smile and wave when they see Zeus. Sam and his mama are there also and have brought games for everyone to play. And Lily and her mom are wearing matching pink coats and pink sparkling hats as they hand out dog biscuits.

Then Miss Molly makes an announcement, thanking all the pups for putting this party together.

"This starts a new year, which means new chances for us to help each other and make the world a better place," she says.

Every paw claps in agreement. Then, fireworks light up the night! The pups have never seen fireworks and are a little scared at first, but then they see how beautiful it is. The pups look up in the night sky to see it exploding with color.

That night, it snows some more, and Zeus stays up a little later than normal with Mama, watching the snow fall outside the window. Zeus gets ready for bed and asks his mama what new things are in store for him the next day.

Mama says, "My little husky pup, you're just going to have to go to sleep and find out tomorrow."

As he goes off to sleep, he closes his eyes and says, "I can't wait for tomorrow."

And he lets out a slight howl.

About the Author...

Heather Marie is the Author of :

- The Adventures of the Panda and the Pug

- The Adventures of the Husky Puppy - Back to School, Puppy Style!

- The Adventures of the Husky Puppy - SNOW DAY!

Email and Social Media List

HeatherMariebooksinc@gmail.com

@heathermariebooksinc   Facebook

@heathermariebooksinc   Instagram

@Heathermbook   Twitter

Made in the USA
Middletown, DE
06 March 2023

26297540R00020